Whose nose?
Whose toes?

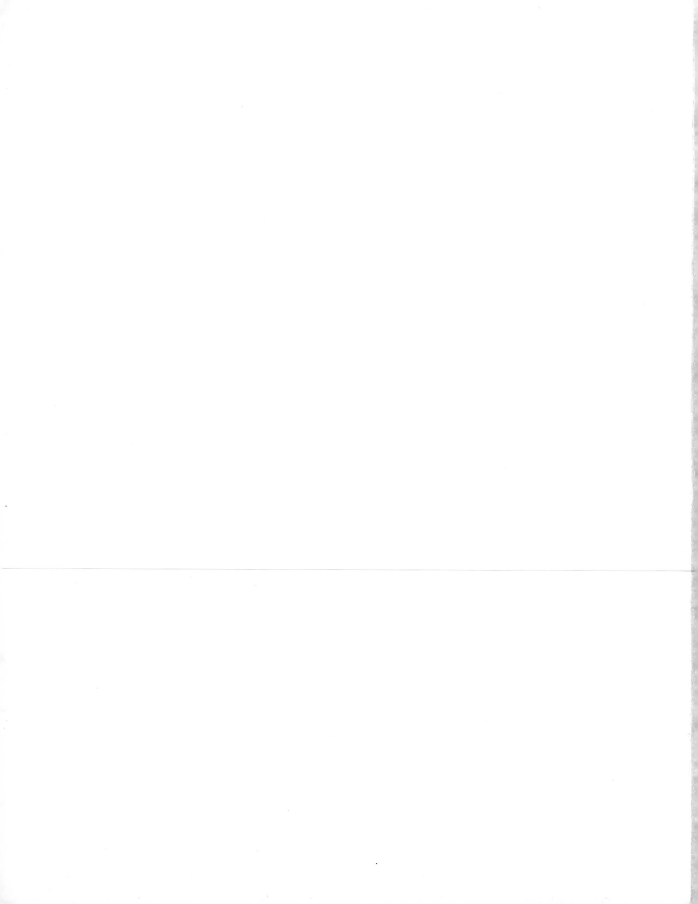

Whose nose?
Whose toes?

Illustrated by Piers Harper

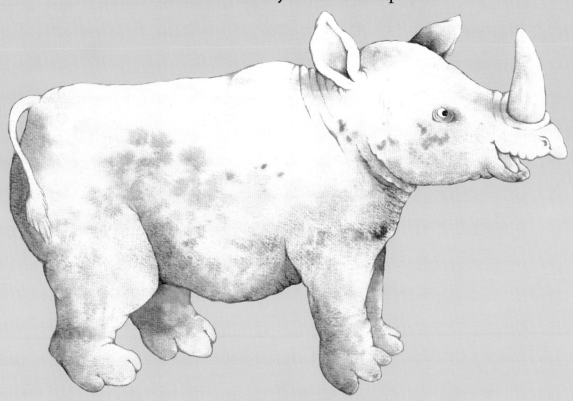

BACKPACKBOOKS

NEW YORK

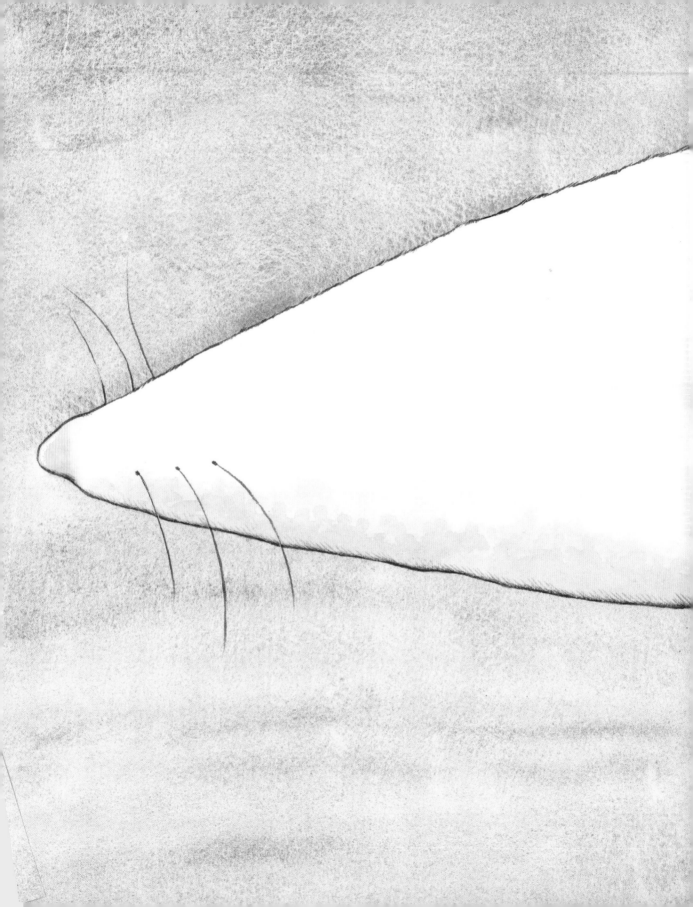

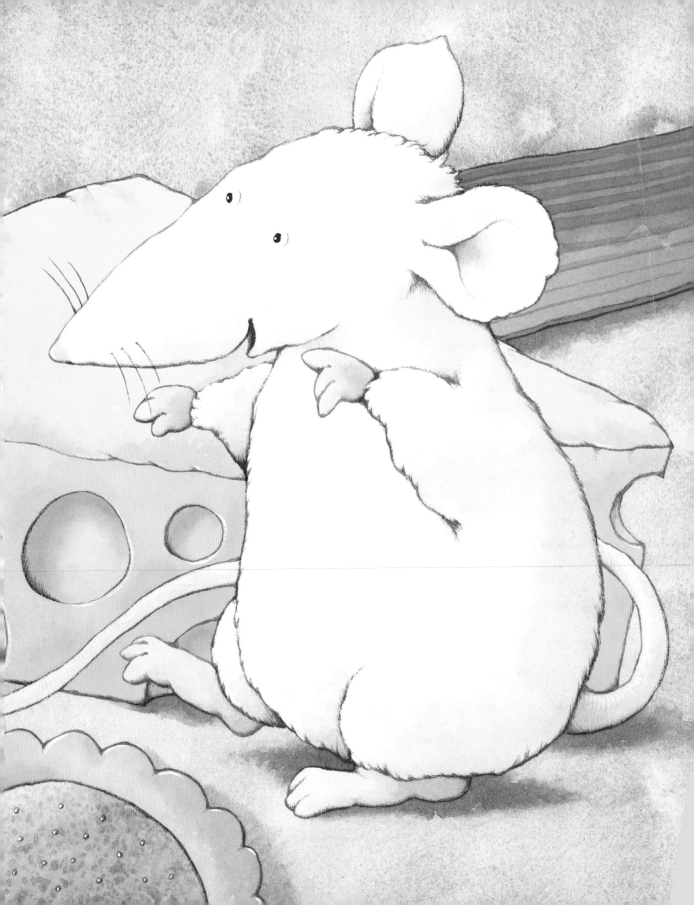

"It's my nose," squeaked the mouse.

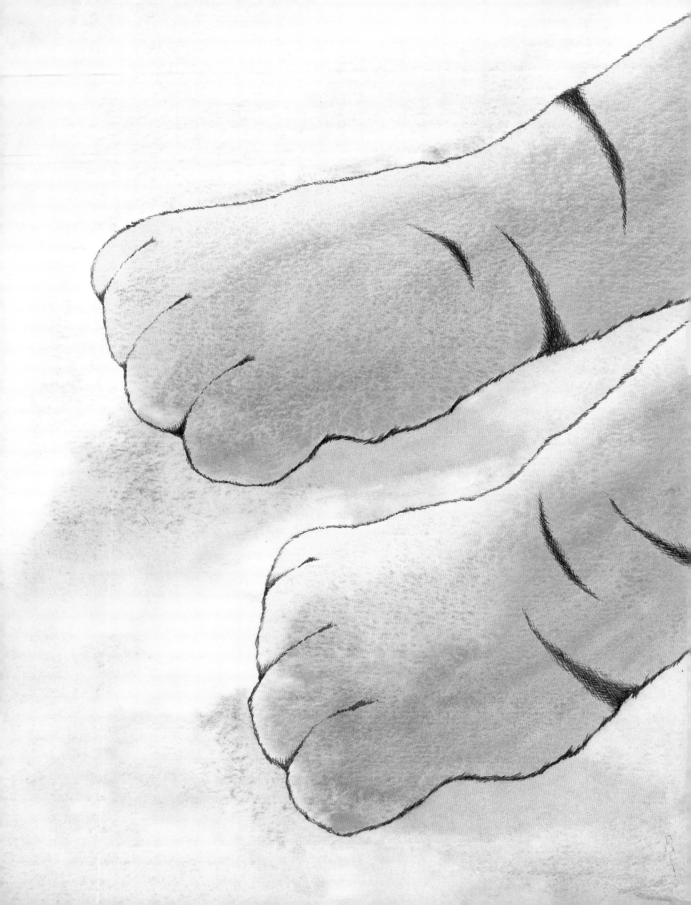

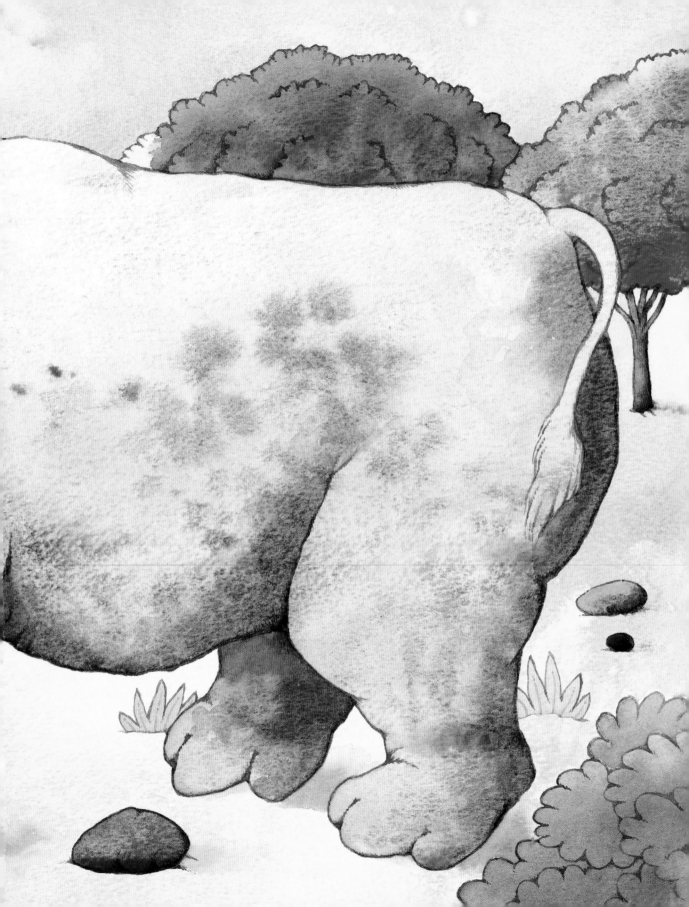

"It's my nose," grumbled the rhinoceros.

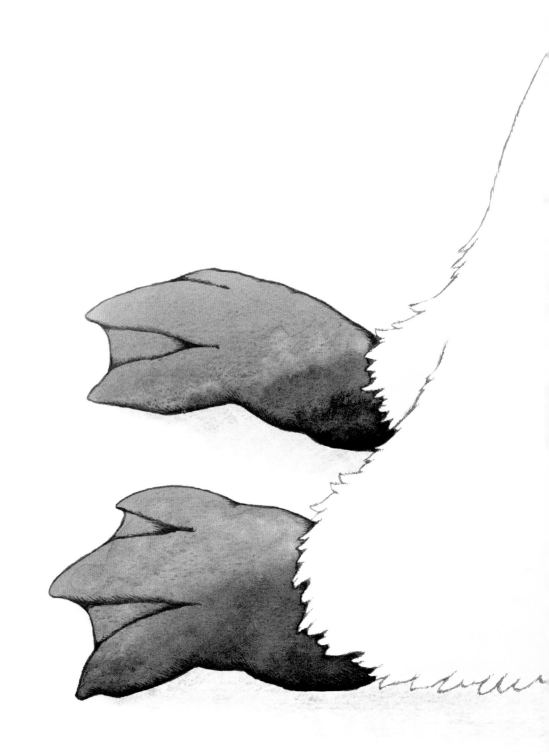

"They're my toes," squawked the penguin.

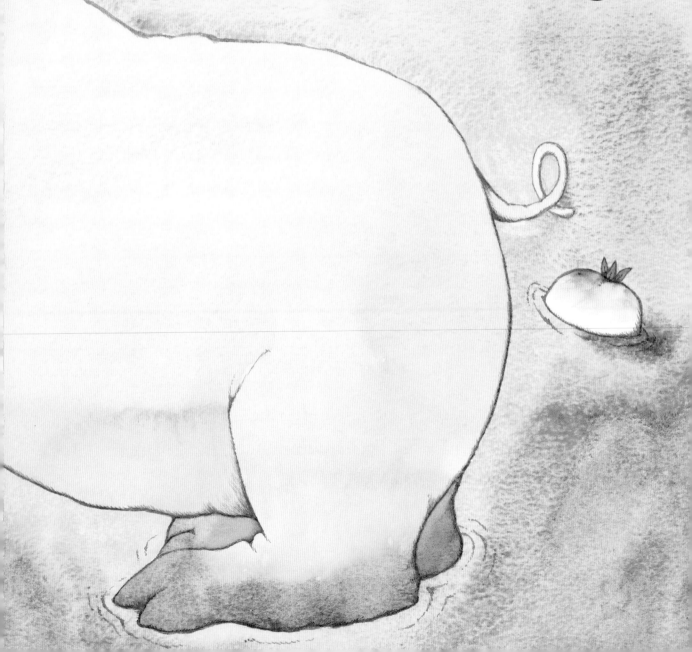

"It's my nose," grunted the pig.

"Whose toes are those?"

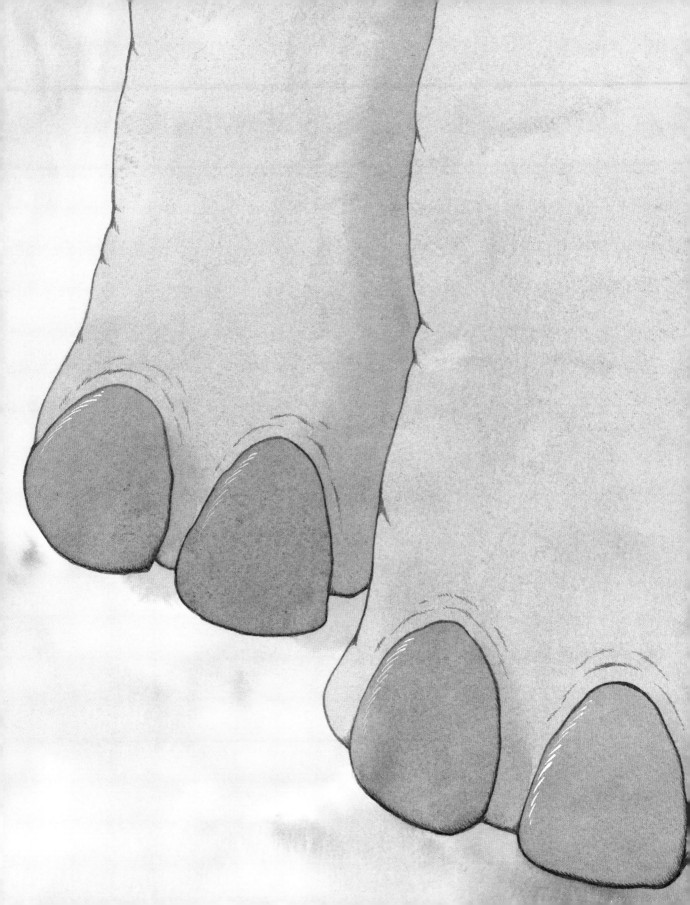

"They're my toes," trumpeted the elephant.

"Whose nose is that?"

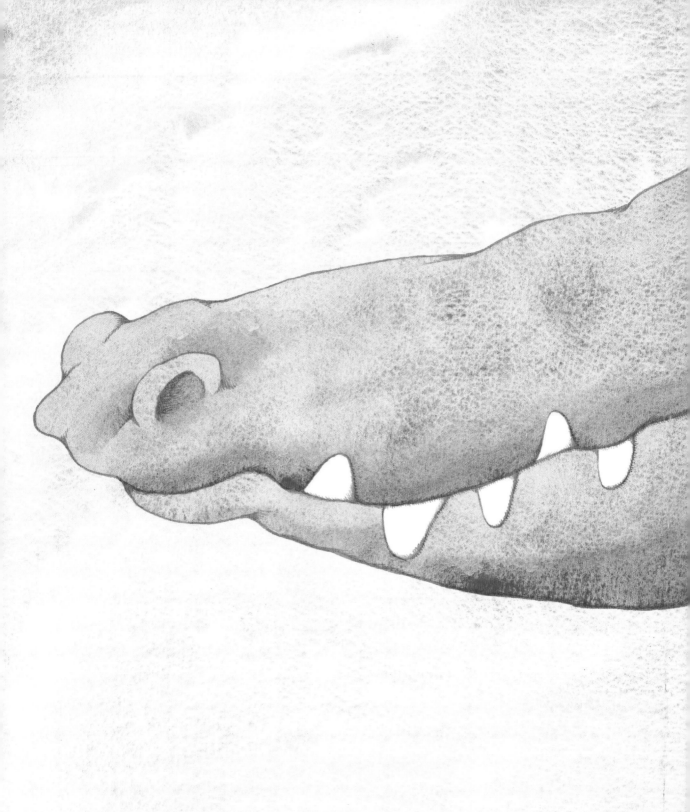

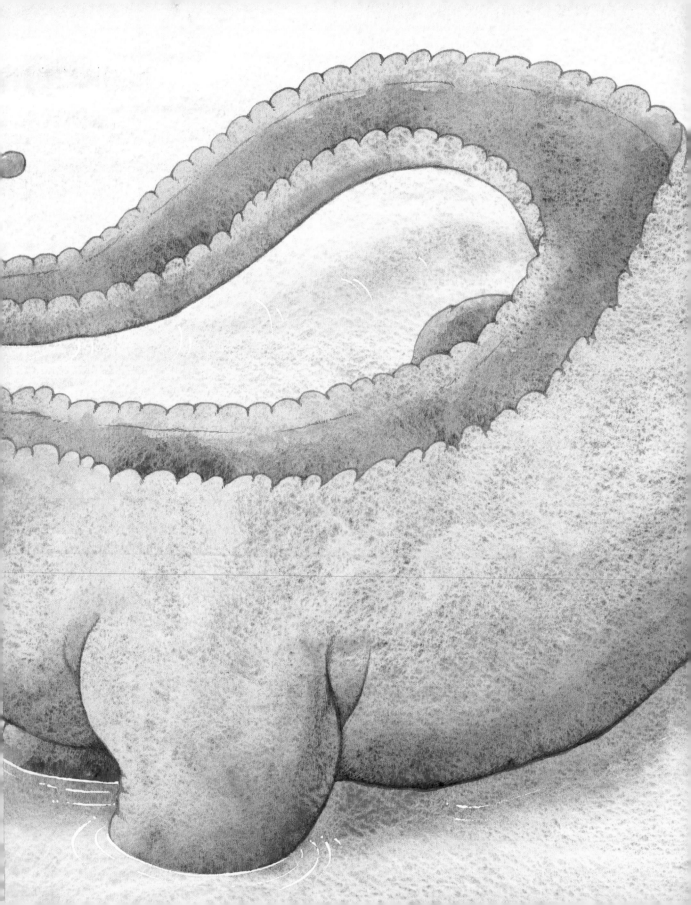

"It's my nose," snapped the crocodile.

Whose toes are those?
Whose nose is that?
It could be a dog,
It could be a cat.
They could be yours,
They could be mine,
You'll have to guess,
we're out of time!